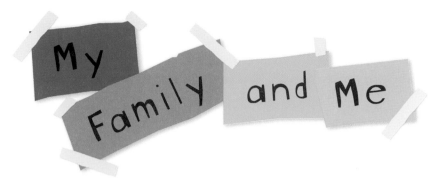

# Going On Vacation

## Mary Auld

SEA-TO-SEA
*Mankato Collingwood London*

Everyone likes to go away on vacation. It's a time to relax and have fun with your family.

**?** Your turn...

Have you been away on vacation with your family? Where did you go?

Sarah and her grandmother decide where to go on vacation together.

Sarah says:

"Grandma and I like to go somewhere hot and sunny."

When it is time to get ready
to go, Lynne and her twin,
Becky, help with the packing.

People travel in different ways to go on vacation. Sometimes we go by car.

Sometimes we go by train or bus. Meera holds Mom's hand tightly at the station.

? Your turn...
What way do you like to travel on vacation?

Sometimes we go away on vacation in an airplane. First, we have to go to the airport.

Then we get on the plane and fly to another airport, often in another state.

Fleur says:
"It's exciting arriving in a new place—even if it's raining!"

Sometimes we visit relatives for a vacation. Duncan loves staying with his grandparents.

Your turn...

Which relatives do you go to stay with? What do you like doing there?

We can go away on vacation just about anywhere. We can visit a big city ...

Neil says:

"We walked more than 3 miles one day—and I didn't complain!"

... or go hiking in the country.

Of course, the best vacations are on a beach.

? Your turn...

Why do you think so many families go to the beach on vacation?

When we're away, we need somewhere to stay. A tent makes a cozy vacation home.

# So does a trailer.

> Gwen says:
> "I love our trailer—it's like taking your home on vacation with you."

Sometimes people stay at a hotel or rent an apartment for the family.

**?** Your turn...

What kind of place would you like to stay in on vacation?

Harry's family found an apartment with its own swimming pool.

On vacation, we take pictures and buy souvenirs.

Back home, we can look at them and remember our trip.

66 Hailey says:

"Grandma and I laugh all over again when we look at the pictures of us playing in the waves."

Where would you like to go on vacation with your family?

# Some Things to Do

With your friends, make a collection of pictures of your family vacations. Tell each other about where you went and what you did.

Plan "the best vacation ever." Where would you go? What would you do? Make a list of what you would need to pack.

Ask your grandparents or parents to tell you about vacations they went on as children. How were they different from today?

Sometimes we spend our vacation at home. Write a story or poem about a vacation where you didn't go anywhere.

## About this book

The aim of this book is to give children the opportunity to explore what their family means to them and their role within it in a positive and celebratory way. In particular it emphasizes the importance of care and support within the family. It also encourages children to compare their own experiences with other people, recognizing similarities and differences and respecting these as part of daily life.

Children will get pleasure out of looking at this book on their own. However, sharing the book on a one-to-one basis or within a group will also be very rewarding. Just talking about the main text and pictures is a good starting point, and the panels also prompt discussion:
• Question panels ask children to talk directly about their own experiences and feelings.
• Quote panels encourage them to think further by comparing their experiences with those of other children.

This edition first published in 2011 by
Sea-to-Sea Publications
Distributed by Black Rabbit Books
P.O. Box 3263, Mankato, Minnesota 56002

Copyright © Sea-to-Sea Publications 2011

Printed in China, Dongguan

Library of Congress Cataloging-in-Publication Data

Auld, Mary.
  Going on vacation / Mary Auld.
      p. cm. -- (My family and me)
  ISBN 978-1-59771-230-9 (library binding)
  1. Family vacations--Juvenile literature. I. Title.
  GV182.8.A95 2011
  790.1'91--dc22

                                    2009051542

9 8 7 6 5 4 3 2

Published by arrangement with the Watts Publishing Group
Ltd, London.


Series editor: Rachel Cooke
Art director: Jonathan Hair
Design: Jason Anscomb

Picture credits: AM Corporation/Alamy: 16. James De
Bounevialle/Photofusion: 13. Kevin Dodge/Corbis: 11. Stan
Gamester/Photofusion: 19. Grace/zefa/Corbis: cover, 8. S & R
Greenhill: 7, 9, 12, 14. LWA-Dann Tardiff/Corbis: 18. David
Montford/Photofusion: 22. Picture Partners/Alamy: 5, 6, 21. Ariel
Skelley/Corbis: 3. Paul Thompson/Corbis: 20. Libby
Welch/Photofusion: 4. Frances Western/Photofusion: 17.
Every attempt has been made to clear copyright. Should there be ὰ
inadvertent omission please apply to the publisher for rectification.

Please note that some of the pictures in this book have been
posed by models.

March 2010
RD/6000006414/002